Frankenstein

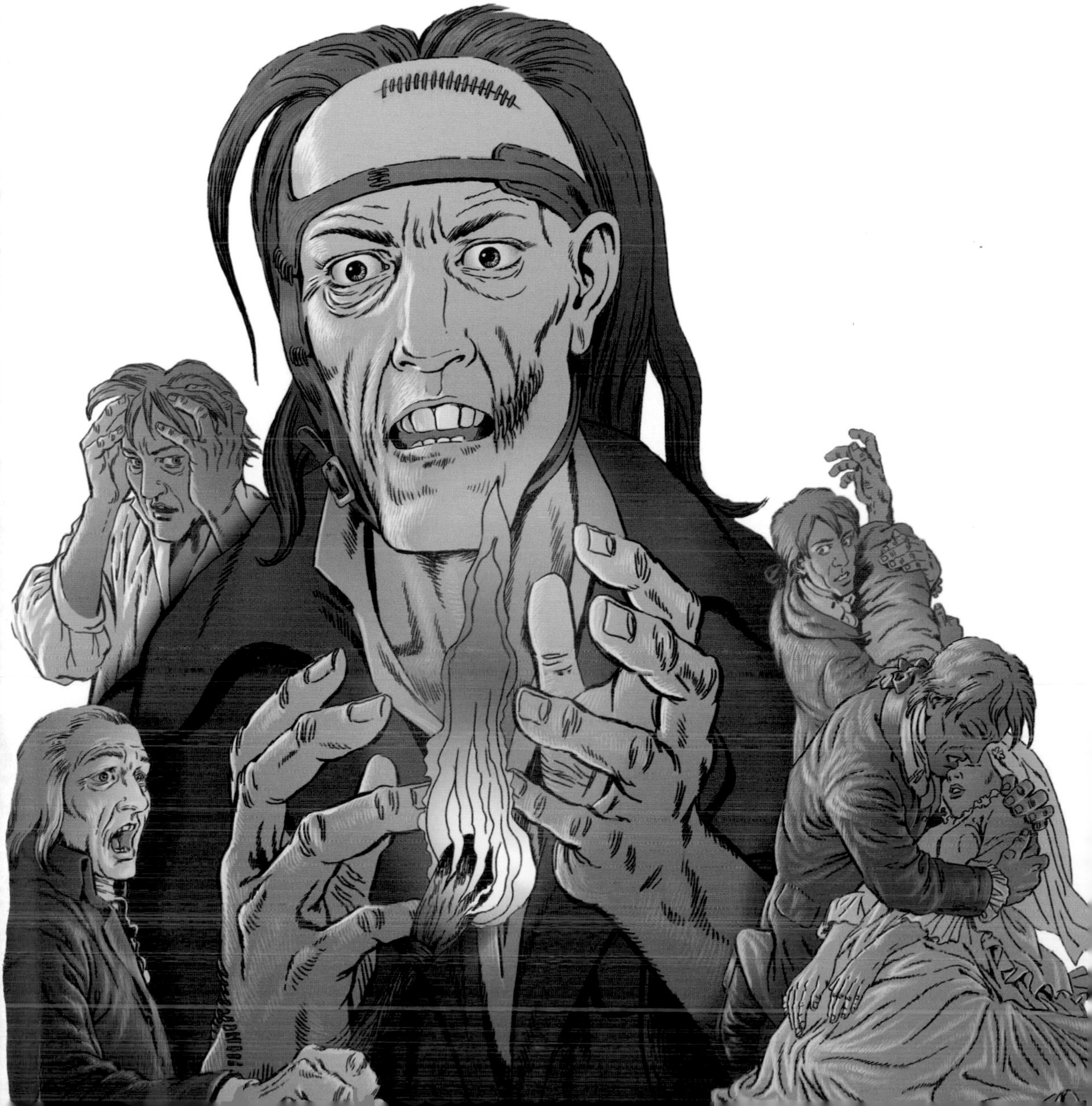

Artists: Penko Gelev
Sotir Gelev

First edition for North America (including Canada and Mexico),
Philippine Islands, and Puerto Rico published in 2008
by Barron's Educational Series, Inc.

All inquiries should be addressed to:
Barron's Educational Series, Inc.
250 Wireless Blvd.
Hauppauge, NY 11788
www.barronseduc.com

ISBN-13 (Hardcover): 978-0-7641-6057-8
ISBN-10 (Hardcover): 0-7641-6057-5
ISBN-13 (Paperback): 978-0-7641-3781-5
ISBN-10 (Paperback): 0-7641-3781-6

Library of Congress Control No.: 2006937854

Picture credits:
p. 40 © 2000 Topham Picturepoint/TopFoto
p. 41 © World History Archive/TopFoto
p. 43 © 2006 Alinari/TopFoto
p. 46 © 2003 Charles Walker/TopFoto
p. 47 © 2003 Topham Picturepoint/TopFoto

Every effort has been made to trace copyright holders. The Salariya Book Company apologizes for
any omissions and would be pleased, in such cases, to add an acknowledgment in future editions.

Printed and bound in China
9 8 7 6 5 4 3 2 1

Frankenstein

Mary Shelley

Illustrated by

Penko Gelev

BARRON'S

Retold by

Fiona Macdonald

Series created and designed by

David Salariya

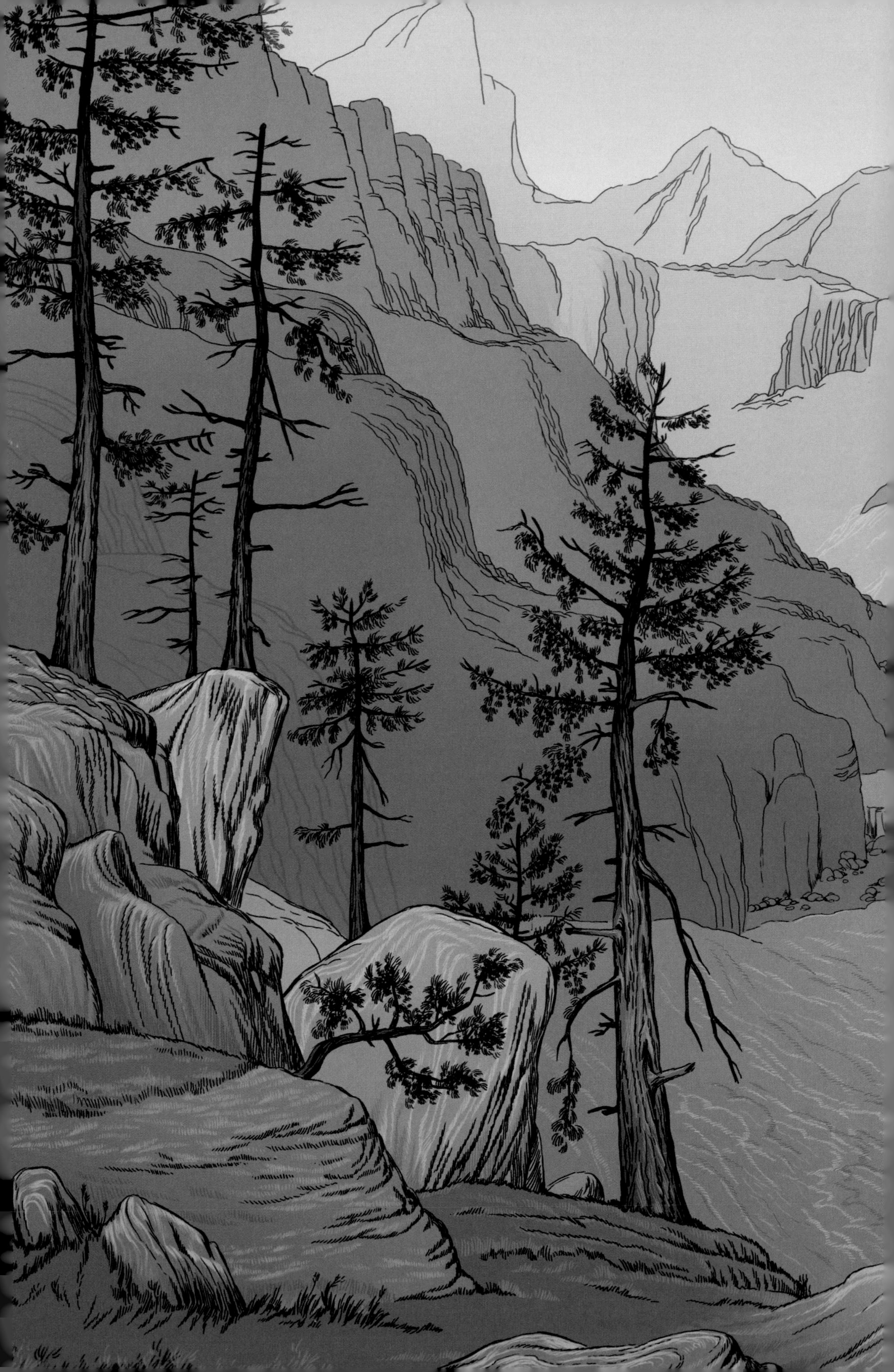

I suddenly beheld the figure of a
man, at some distance, advancing
toward me with superhuman speed.
He bounded over the crevices in the
ice. His stature, also, seemed to
exceed that of a man. I was troubled:
a mist came over my eyes, and I felt a
faintness seize me. I perceived, as the
shape came nearer, that it was
the wretch whom I had created.
I trembled with rage and horror.

"Devil," I exclaimed, "do you dare
approach me?"

(See page 23)

CHARACTERS

Victor Frankenstein,
science student

The Creature

Elizabeth Lavenza,
an orphan

Alphonse Frankenstein,
Victor's father,
a city governor of Geneva

Caroline Frankenstein,
Victor's mother

Ernest Frankenstein,
Victor's teenage brother

William Frankenstein,
Victor's youngest brother

Justine Moritz,
a servant of the
Frankensteins

Henry Clerval,
Victor's
best friend

Mr. de Lacey,
an elderly
nobleman

Felix and Agatha
de Lacey,
his teenage
children

Safie,
girlfriend of Felix

Robert Walton,
Arctic explorer

STRANGE MEETING

July 1799: Near the North Pole

Arctic explorer Robert Walton is writing to his sister. A few days before, gazing out over the frozen sea, he saw a huge figure driving a dogsled.

What could it be? A monster? A ghost? A nightmare?

The next day, Walton's crew found a man floating on the ice, speechless and shivering. They carried him on board…

…and tried to make him eat. But they didn't think he'd survive: he was so cold, so weak, so feeble.

The stranger lay unconscious for days. When finally he opened his eyes, his gaze was wild, mad, suffering.

To seek one who fled from me.

The sailors asked him why he'd risked his life on the ice. They were startled by his reply.

I fancy we have seen him.

I have lost everything…

Walton told the stranger about the huge creature on the ice. The stranger became excited but then broke down, sobbing wildly.

Hear me—let me reveal my tale.

When his strength had returned a little, he asked Walton to listen to his amazing story—a terrible, tragic tale…

Happy Family

Geneva, Switzerland

The stranger is called Victor; his family name is Frankenstein. His father, Alphonse, was a city governor, rich, hard-working, respected by all.

An old friend of Alphonse's has lost all his money. Alphonse hunts for him, and, at long last, finds him.

The friend is sick and starving. His daughter Caroline looks after him and earns money by making straw hats. Alphonse sends help, but it is too late—his friend dies.

Two years later

I do!

I do!

Alphonse marries Caroline. They're very happy, but Caroline is not strong. She needs rest, good food, and sunshine.

A land of wonders!

Venice, Italy

Together, they travel to warmer, sunnier lands. Thanks to the mild weather, a comfortable life—and Alphonse's tender care—Caroline grows stronger.

He's bestowed[1] by Heaven!

Victor, their first son, is born on their travels. They are full of joy—but Caroline longs for a daughter as well.

Caroline often gives poor families food, drink, or clothing. She wants to share her good fortune. In one house, she meets a little girl—an orphan.

Pretty Elizabeth!

Caroline brings the orphan girl home to be part of the Frankenstein family. Everyone adores her.

1. bestowed: sent as a gift.

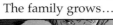

The family grows…

…and moves back to Switzerland.

The Philosopher's Stone[1] . . . the Elixir of Life![2]

Elizabeth and Victor are best friends. They play and have lessons together.

Their classmate, Henry Clerval, plays with them. He likes fighting and adventure stories. They like investigating wildlife.

Victor finds dusty old books in a corner of his father's study—full of magic, mysterious and exciting!

Do not waste your time upon this; it is sad trash.

…to uncover the secrets of Nature!

Alphonse says they are full of nonsense. Victor does not want to believe him.

He dreams of being a magic scientist with a thrilling secret quest.

He wants to find the force that makes things live. He puzzles: why do plants—and people— die, but rocks survive forever?

CRACK!

One day, Victor sees a mighty tree blasted by lightning. What amazing power is hidden in the storm? A scientist friend explains about electricity.

Is this a clue to Victor's quest? He must find out more! If electricity can kill—can it also bring life back again?

1. Philosopher's Stone: a magic substance supposed to turn ordinary metal into gold.
2. Elixir of Life: a magic potion supposed to make people live forever.

LEAVING HOME

Victor is going to study science at Ingolstadt University in Germany.

But tragedy strikes. Elizabeth falls ill and everyone fears she will die. Caroline nurses her back to health…

My children!

…then catches the same fever herself. She dies calmly; her last wish is that Victor and Elizabeth should marry.

I regret that I am taken from you.

Victor's stunned. He simply can't believe that his mother is dead.

Elizabeth does her best to comfort the grieving Frankenstein family. There are now three brothers: Victor, Ernest, and William, who is still a baby.

Many weeks later:

Farewell!

Henry Clerval says that he longs to go to university, like Victor. But his father won't let him: Henry must start work in his family's business. It's good-bye!

Alone!

Victor's still mourning his mother. He'd really like a friend with him right now. Gloomily, and with a mind full of fears, he sets off for university.

Ingolstadt, Germany

By the time Victor arrives, he's feeling much better. But, alone in his room, he thinks longingly of his family and worries about the future.

Have you really spent your time in studying such nonsense?

Next day, Victor goes to see the professors who'll be teaching him. They are very scornful of the dusty old books he's been reading.

You must begin your studies anew!

I will unfold[1] to the world the deepest mysteries of creation!

But Professor Waldman, a chemist, is much more helpful. He talks about the real-life miracles of science.

Waldman's teaching inspires Victor with an awesome new ambition.

1. unfold: discover and explain.

THE MEANING OF LIFE

Two years pass.

Victor forgets all about his family back home. He's utterly obsessed with studying. He stays up all day and all night, reading and making experiments.

Good!

Victor learns quickly; his professors are pleased. But he doesn't tell them all he's doing. Secretly, he's cutting up dead bodies to try to find where their life force comes from.

So brilliant and wondrous, yet so simple!

Victor gets rotting corpses from graveyards and tombs. Slowly, carefully, he observes how dead bodies decay. He studies living creatures too…

…and finally finds what he's searching for: the secret of life itself!

Could I give life to an animal as wonderful as man?

But Victor can't rest. He has another problem: the life force he's discovered needs a flesh-and-blood body to live in.

Victor works in a secret study on the top floor of his apartment. He's decided to make a gigantic figure, about 8 feet (2.4 meters) tall.

A new species will bless me as its creator!

After frantic, sleepless months spent sawing, cutting, and stitching…

The horrors of my secret work!

…Victor's exhausted. But he can't stop now. He must go on!

On a dreary night in November, Victor's work is completed.

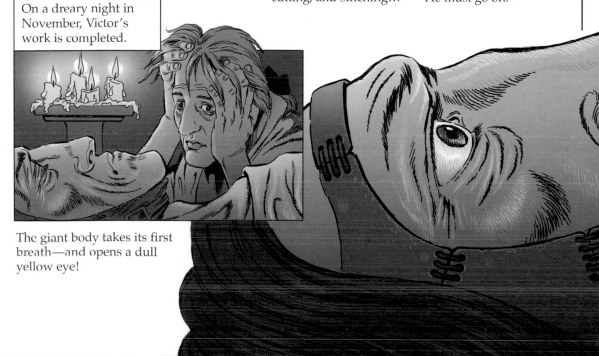

The giant body takes its first breath—and opens a dull yellow eye!

THE CREATURE LIVES!

Victor's appalled. He's worked so hard, and now his dream's a nightmare!

He'd hoped to build a beautiful body… but he's created a monster!

Horrified by the hideous creature he has made, Victor flees from the room.

He paces up and down his bedroom until he is completely exhausted.

At last he collapses on the bed. But his sleep is haunted by scary, sickening visions…

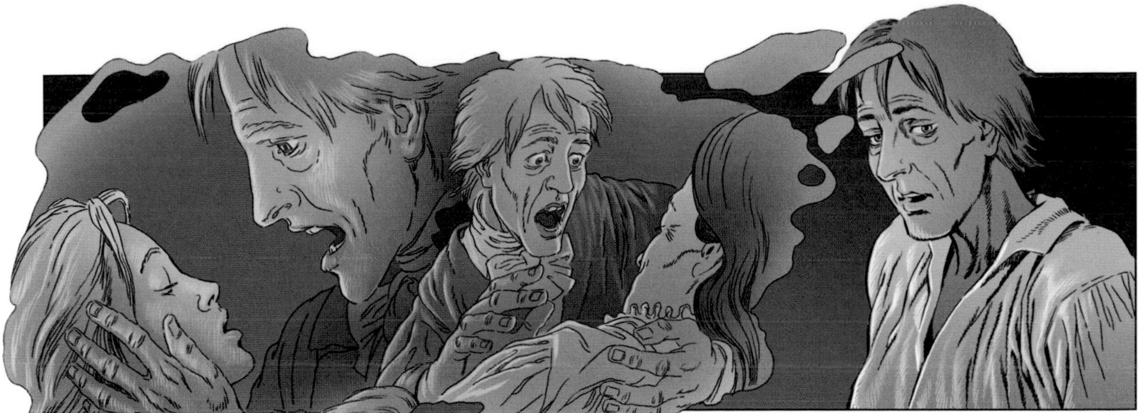

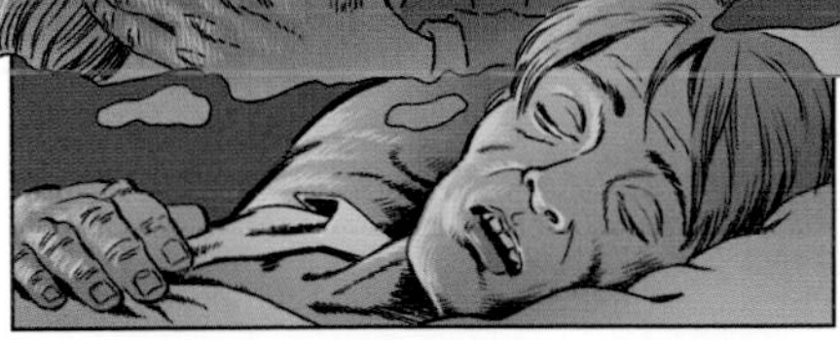

In his dream he sees his dear, sweet Elizabeth, and hurries to kiss her. But she turns into his dead mother's corpse, rotting and crawling with worms!

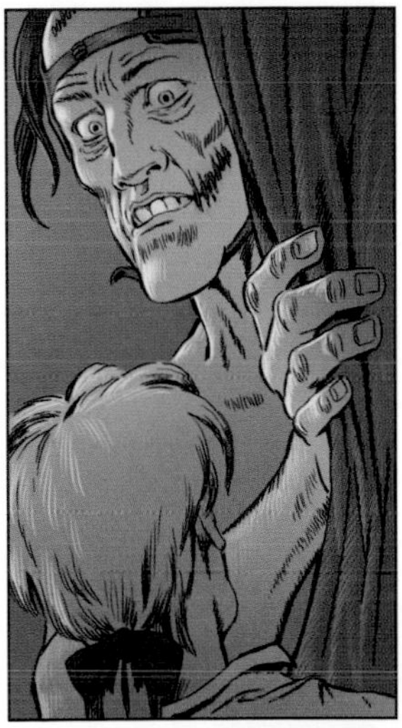

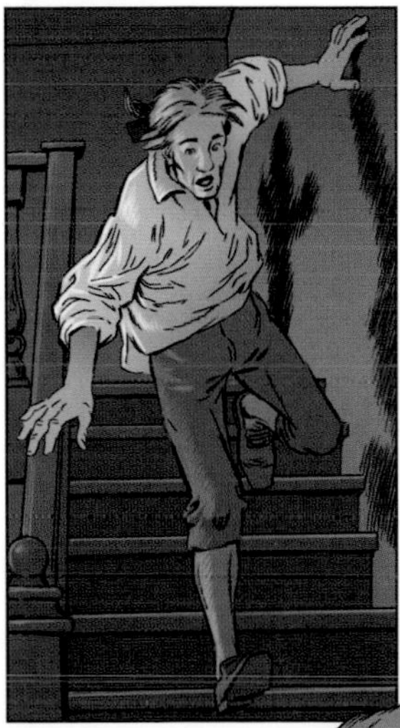

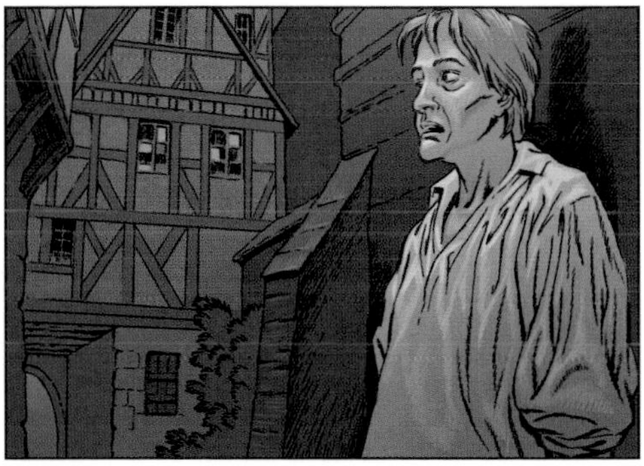

Victor wakes to find a huge, clumsy hand reaching through the bed curtains. He dashes out of the house, his heart thumping wildly.

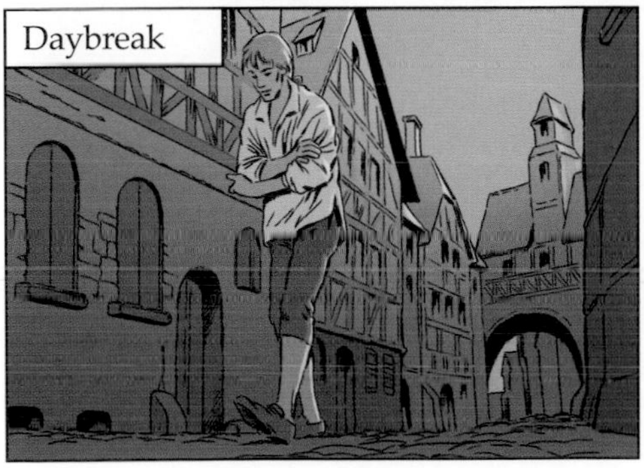
Daybreak

He staggers though the streets in the pouring rain, half-crazy. He doesn't know where he's going, but he doesn't dare go back.

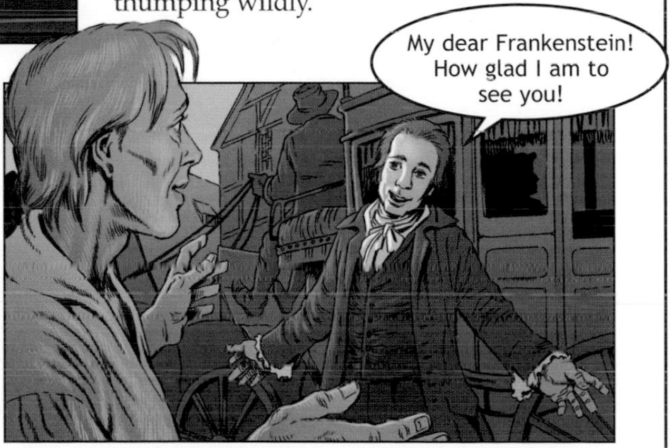
My dear Frankenstein! How glad I am to see you!

By chance he finds himself outside an inn, where a coach has arrived from Switzerland. He stops to look—and finds himself staring straight at his old friend, Henry Clerval!

DISAPPEARED!

> How ill you appear! So thin and pale!

Victor can hardly believe his luck—fate has sent a friend to help him, just when he needed it most! He is so pleased to see Henry that he nearly bursts into tears.

Henry has left his job. He's going to be a student… But then he stops talking, and looks closely at Victor. What on earth is the matter with him?

Back at Victor's apartment

Frightful visions of the Creature swirl around Victor's brain. But he didn't dare tell Henry what he's been doing. He asks Henry to wait, then rushes up to his study.

> A few minutes…

Thank goodness—the room is empty!

It's safe for Henry to come upstairs.

> How ill you are!

> Oh, save me! Save me!

Victor sighs with relief, then starts to laugh—strangely, wildly, madly. He imagines that the Creature is with them in the room, ready to attack him! Henry is shocked at his behavior.

He seems to feel the monster's huge hands closing around his throat—and falls to the floor, unconscious.

The monster... the monster...

"My dearest! Get well— and return to us!"

Victor's ill—very ill. He's slumped in bed, almost lifeless. Henry looks after him, but cannot understand. What has caused Victor's madness?

Victor's troubled mind is haunted by visions of his Creature. Henry is alarmed by his shouts and screams.

Slowly and painfully, Victor gets better. He can think, speak, and read again. Henry gives him a letter that has just arrived. It's from Elizabeth.

Astonishing progress!

Victor will do as Elizabeth says: go home and spend time with his family. Before he leaves, the professors congratulate him on his work. But, deep inside, he's still full of fear.

Warm sun... a garden of roses...

Victor must wait until spring to cross the mountains into Switzerland. To pass the time, he reads poetry. Compared with science, it's very soothing!

17

WHO KILLED WILLIAM?

At last, Victor begins to feel healthy, strong, and cheerful.

He and Henry enjoy a walking holiday in the hills.

But, when they get back to Ingolstadt, a terrible shock awaits them!

William is dead! He is murdered!

There's a letter from Alphonse. Victor reads it with horror.

The letter explains…

One fine evening, the Frankenstein family went for a stroll in the woods. Ernest and William ran ahead, playing hide-and-seek.

I waited for him a long time.

A little while later, Ernest came back, looking worried and frightened. Had anyone seen William? Ernest couldn't find him anywhere!

WILLIAM!

WILLIAM!

The Frankensteins hurried back to the house. But William wasn't there! What could have happened? How could he have disappeared? Desperately, fearfully, they searched the woods again.

WILLIAM!

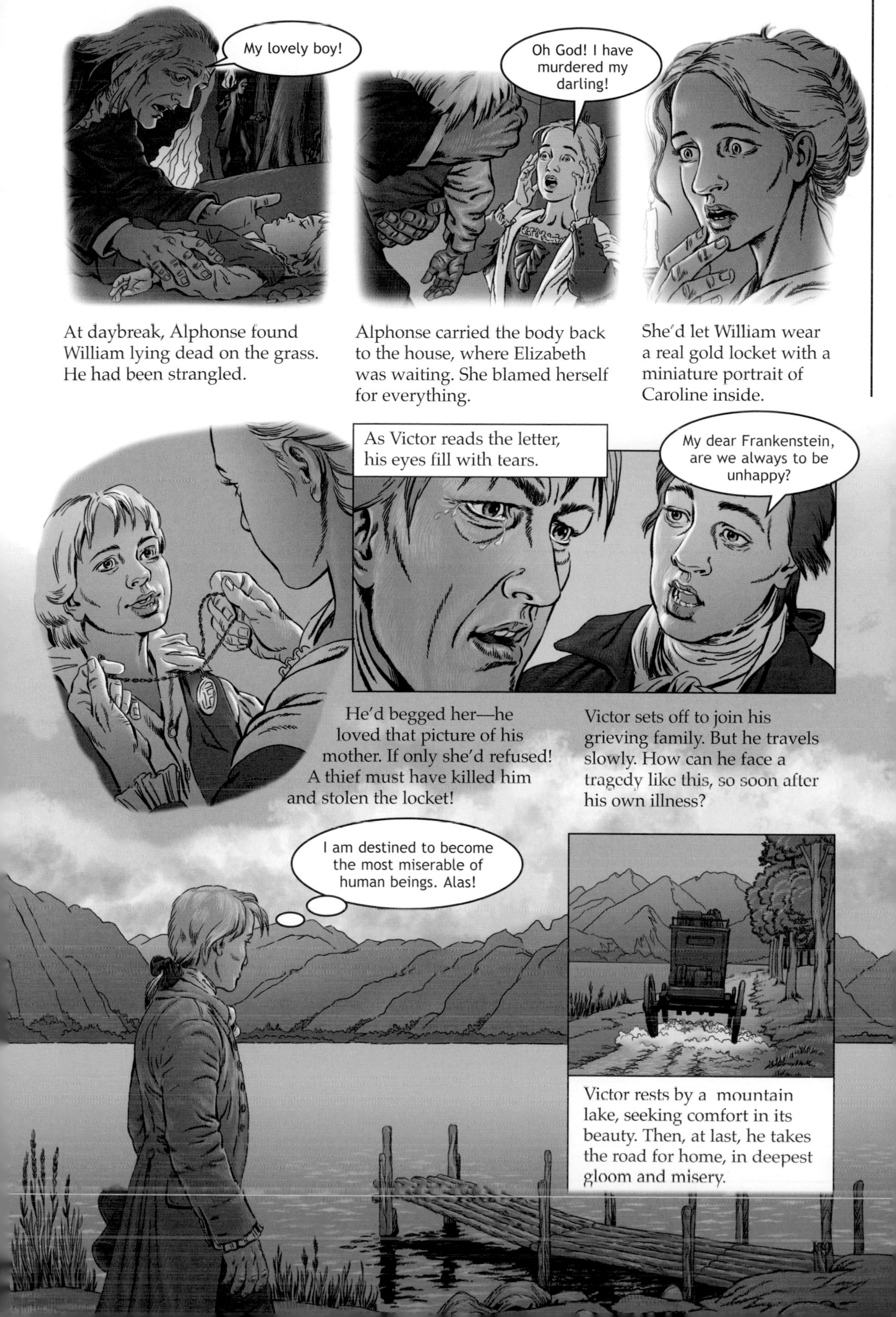
My lovely boy!
At daybreak, Alphonse found William lying dead on the grass. He had been strangled.
Oh God! I have murdered my darling!
Alphonse carried the body back to the house, where Elizabeth was waiting. She blamed herself for everything.
She'd let William wear a real gold locket with a miniature portrait of Caroline inside.
He'd begged her—he loved that picture of his mother. If only she'd refused! A thief must have killed him and stolen the locket!
As Victor reads the letter, his eyes fill with tears.
My dear Frankenstein, are we always to be unhappy?
Victor sets off to join his grieving family. But he travels slowly. How can he face a tragedy like this, so soon after his own illness?
I am destined to become the most miserable of human beings. Alas!
Victor rests by a mountain lake, seeking comfort in its beauty. Then, at last, he takes the road for home, in deepest gloom and misery.

INNOCENT VICTIM

Victor rows across the lake toward home.

William, dear angel! This is thy[1] funeral, this thy dirge![2]

Night falls, and a violent thunderstorm rages in the mountains. To Victor, it seems as if all of Nature is mourning William's murder.

Victor takes shelter. He's alone with his memories of William. But then a sudden flash of lightning shows a dark figure, peering around a tree.

Horrified, Victor recognizes the Creature he has made. In a flash, he understands the terrible truth: it was his Creature that killed William!

Nothing in human shape could have destroyed that fair child. *He* was the murderer!

Poor William! He was our darling and our pride!

The murderer has been discovered.

Good God! How can that be? He was free last night!

I do not know what you mean.

Victor spends all night in the woods, in utter misery. Has he made a Creature that can only harm and kill?

At daybreak, Victor hurries to his family house. Ernest, now his only living brother, greets him.

Ernest tells of the Frankenstein family's shock and anguish. Then he adds some astonishing news.

No one would believe it at first,

and even now Elizabeth will not be convinced.

Ernest does not understand what Victor is trying to say, and continues his story. The murderer, it seems, is Justine, the family's trusted servant!

The whole town—except Elizabeth and Victor—thinks that Justine killed young William. Her trial begins today. The whole family must go.

---

1. thy: a loving or friendly way of saying "your."
2. dirge: a sad funeral song.

> God knows I am innocent.

> WILLIAM!

Victor swears that Justine cannot be the murderer. But he dare not mention his Creature, so no one believes him.

Justine tells how she helped to search for William until late at night, when she fell asleep in a barn, cold, wet, and exhausted. Next morning, she returned home—and learned that William was dead. She was devastated.

> I believe in her perfect innocence.

A servant put her to bed—and found the locket hidden in her clothes. Justine doesn't know how it got there.

Elizabeth still believes that Justine is not guilty. Bravely, she tells the court how much she trusts and admires her. Justine's a loyal servant—and a good, kind, helpful, honest person.

> This was my doing—all the work of my thrice-accursed[1] hands!

> Unhappy ones— these are not your last tears!

Despite Elizabeth's passionate plea, the trial verdict is "Guilty!" Victor begs the judge to show mercy—but he refuses. Justine must hang!

Before she dies, Justine confesses to the murder. She is not guilty, but she wants the church to forgive her sins so she'll join William in Heaven. Elizabeth is heartbroken.

1. Thrice-accursed: three-times cursed.

FACE TO FACE

I have committed deeds beyond description.

Do you think, Victor, that I do not suffer also?

No one could love a child more than I loved your brother.

The Frankensteins mourn two innocent victims: William and Justine. All the time, Victor is tormented by feelings of guilt and shame. He hates himself.

Victor's father urges him to control his feelings, like a man. It's Victor's duty to be brave, and comfort the rest of his family.

Now misery has come home.

I am tempted to plunge into the silent lake, that the waters might close over me and my torment forever.

The sight of Victor's sorrowing family is more than he can bear. He keeps away from them as much as he can.

He spends hours in his boat, alone. How can he end his misery?

I ardently wish to extinguish that life.[1]

Perhaps exercise will calm Victor's mind. He sets off for the high mountains.

I seek to forget myself and my sorrows.

But Victor must stay alive, to protect his family from the Creature. The thought of it makes him grind his teeth. He dreams of hunting and killing it.

1. I ardently . . . life: I long to kill the Creature.

The mountains are immense, magnificent, awe-inspiring. They make Victor think about God, and forget about the terrible Creature.

But then he spies a fearsome figure bounding toward him across the ice!

I cease to fear!

Devil! Do you dare approach me? Begone—or stay, that I may trample you to dust!

Oh, if only I could restore those victims you have so diabolically[1] murdered!

I expected this reception. All men hate the wretched—and I am miserable beyond all living things!

For days, Victor climbs high into the valley and across the glacier. He's exhausted, but at peace—too tired to worry.

The tortures of Hell are too mild a sentence for thy crimes!

Let your compassion be moved,[5] and do not disdain[6] me.

Remember that I am thy creature.[2] I was benevolent[3] and good;

misery made me a fiend. Make me happy, and I shall again be virtuous.[4]

Listen to my tale...

The Creature, like Victor, has found refuge in the wild, remote mountains. Victor curses the Creature in fury, but the Creature is just as angry with him.

The Creature blames his own murderous behavior on Victor's unkindness. If only the Creature had been loved and cared for, he would have loved Victor in return.

1. diabolically: devilishly.
2. I am thy creature: you created me.
3. benevolent: kind.
4. virtuous: good
5. Let your compassion be moved: Take pity on me.
6. disdain: scorn.

23

THE CREATURE'S TALE

The Creature speaks…

When I left the room where I was made, I couldn't make sense of what I saw, felt, or heard. I sat down and wept. Slowly I began to understand my surroundings.

I observed the sun and moon, the trees and leaves, and heard the birds sing. I found a fire left by travellers, and learned to cook food on it.

Winter came. I was shivering and hungry. I left my forest hideout to look for somewhere warmer. I found a shepherd's hut—but the shepherd ran away.

I saw houses. I smelled food. I went closer, and stepped into one of the buildings. The woman inside shrieked and fainted—and the villagers chased me away.

I climbed up the mountain, away from the village, until I found an old cottage with a covered pigsty outside.

The sty was cramped, but warm and dry. I hid there all day, peering into the cottage.

I could see three people: an old man, a young man, and a girl. Their speech and manners were gracious, but they looked poor.

My sweet Arabian!

Sometimes the father, who was blind, sang and played his guitar. I listened in wonder— I'd never heard music.

Felix and Agatha worked hard, growing vegetables, fetching water, cooking and cleaning. I helped them secretly by bringing wood for their fire.

One day, a beautiful stranger arrived. Felix was delighted! She was the daughter of a Muslim merchant he had helped, years ago, in France.

Safie (that was her name) had run away to find Felix, and marry him. The old man gave them his blessing. I saw their joy, but could not share it—*I* had no family!

Safie did not speak the same language as the others. So Felix and his father taught her. Secretly, I also listened and learned, safely hidden in my pigsty.

Who am I? What am I?

Accursed[1] creator! Why did you form a monster so hideous?

Soon I could speak very well, and read. The books I found made me think, and ask questions. In the coat that I took from your study, Victor, I found an old notebook of yours. It recorded how you designed me, assembled me, created me… and hated me!

1. Accursed: cursed, damned.

THE TALE CONTINUES

I learned that I was not like ordinary people. My reflection in a stream taught me that I looked horrible.

But I was lonely, and wanted friends to share my life. I decided to ask the old man for help. He could not see, so my looks would not scare him.

I waited until one day he was alone, then I went into his cottage. The old man welcomed me kindly. Yes, he would be my friend!

But then Felix, Agatha, and Safie walked in. I have never seen such a panic! Safie ran away, Agatha fell to the floor in a faint—and Felix attacked me!

He grabbed the largest stick he could find, and beat me over the head. Cursing him—and you too, Victor!—I ran away.

All night I paced up and down through the woods, raging like a wild beast.

How dare humans treat other creatures so cruelly? All I wanted was friendship!

Next day I crept back to the cottage. The whole family was leaving. I waited until they had gone, then set fire to their home. It was destroyed—completely!

1. spurned: rejected.

The whole wide world lay before me. But where should I go? I decided to find you, Victor—my creator!

I spent weeks wandering through woods and mountains, out of sight of humans. But one day I found a young girl—drowning!

I rescued her—but her ungrateful friends shot at me with guns. I was badly wounded.

I hid for weeks, in dreadful pain—and full of burning anger.

At last, I reached the woods near your home, and met a boy playing. At first I hoped he'd be a friend, but I learned he was your brother. So I took revenge on you for creating me—by destroying him!

A gold locket glittered on his dead body. I took it and opened it.

I saw a lovely portrait: your mother, I believe. My heart was touched— *I* wanted a woman to love and care for, too!

I came to the barn where Justine slept. She was beautiful—but I knew she would not love me. So I punished her by hiding the locket in her dress. People would think she murdered the boy!

1. vengeance: revenge.

MAKE ME A WIFE!

Victor is horrified by the Creature's story.

But the Creature has more to say. Now that he's met a happy family and seen a beautiful woman, he cannot bear to live alone. He wants to give and receive care, tenderness, love.

I demand it of you as a right.

He asks Victor to make a female creature to be his wife. He promises that they would live far away, in a wild, empty land, where they would harm nobody.

Shall I create another like yourself, whose joint wickedness might desolate[1] the world?

Victor is appalled by the idea.

Oh! my creator, make me happy! I am malicious[2] because I am miserable.

If I cannot inspire love, I will cause fear.

Have a care: I will work at your destruction. You shall curse the hour of your birth!

1. desolate: ruin.
2. malicious: cruel, evil.

28

With a great effort, the Creature calms down.

There is some justice in his argument.

Our lives will not be happy, but they will be harmless, and free from misery.

What I ask of you is reasonable and moderate; do not deny my request!

Leave Europe forever, and every other place in the neighborhood of man.

Begin your work. When you are ready I shall appear.

At last, Victor agrees to make a monster wife for the Creature—on one condition.

Delighted, the Creature promises, and bounds away down the mountainside. Victor watches him go, with a heavy heart. His mind's in a whirl. Should he keep his promise, or should he kill himself?

Let me become as nought.[1]

I have no right to claim their sympathies.

At home, the next day, he can hardly speak. The others are worried about him. But to Victor they seem like ghosts in a dream. Only his new task is real.

1. nought: nothing.

29

ENGLISH EXPERTS

I cannot gather the courage.

Weeks pass, and Victor has still not started to make the female monster. He fears the Creature will be disappointed, and soon seek revenge.

He tells himself that he needs more time to study. He decides to go to England, to consult experts there.

I have always looked forward to your marriage.

Victor's father thinks he looks more cheerful, and takes him to one side. He has something important to say: it's time for Victor and Elizabeth to wed!

I love Elizabeth tenderly.

I must let the monster depart with his mate before I enjoy peace.

But Victor can't plan for a happy, peaceful future until he's finished the new monster. Only then can he be sure the Creature won't attack his family.

My dear Frankenstein, this is what it is to live![1] Now I enjoy existence!

Victor's father is disappointed by the delay. Elizabeth tries to hide her sadness. Of course, Victor cannot tell them the real reason for going to England. They ask Henry Clerval to travel with Victor, to make sure that he is safe. Henry's kind, helpful, and cheerful—the ideal travelling companion.

London

Together, the friends view fine scenery and visit important buildings. But only Henry is enjoying himself.

Henry visits writers, artists, and travellers. Victor meets English scientists who promise to help him. Henry notices how sorrowful he is, but does not know why.

Welcome!

1. This is what it is to live!: This is how to enjoy life.

I could pass my life here among these mountains.

The Scottish Highlands

The experts are happy to share their discoveries with Victor. He can't continue without their help. But he hates the work.

After several months in London, Victor and Henry visit Scotland. It's a beautiful country, with high mountains, bright rivers, and ancient castles.

I feel as if I had committed some great crime.

Enjoy yourself! I may be absent for a month or two.

Edinburgh

But Victor cannot enjoy it. All the time, he worries about his family back in Geneva. Are they safe and happy—or is the Creature attacking them?

Victor needs peace and quiet to finish making the monster. He leaves Henry and goes to the Orkney Isles, off Scotland's wild north coast.

Orkney

Orkney's a bleak, rough place, but it suits Victor's mood. He sets up his laboratory there, and gets to work—reluctantly. But Victor's heart is not in the work.

He feels sick, disgusted—and guilty. He walks along the cliffs for hours, gazing out to sea. Every moment, he fears that the Creature might appear.

MIDNIGHT VISITOR

Have I a right to inflict this curse upon everlasting generations?

It is a chilly, moonlit night.

My heart fails within me.

Victor can't sleep. He sits in his laboratory, thinking of all the dreadful things the Creature has done. What if the female monster turns out to be as bad—or worse? What if she won't marry the Creature, or falls in love with a human? What if the two creatures breed savage children to destroy the world?

A ghastly face appears at the window. There is no escape! The Creature has been following him all the time, to make sure that he keeps his promise.

Seeing the Creature's evil expression, Victor makes up his mind. He can't create another monster! He snatches up his knife and hacks the unfinished female to pieces.

AAARGH!

With a howl of devilish despair and revenge, the Creature runs away into the night.

Do you dare to break your promise?

Trembling, terrified, Victor swears he will never create another monster. Hours pass. Then, in the silence, he hears the sound of a boat. The door opens and the furious Creature storms into the room.

"Do you dare destroy my hopes?"

"Never will I create another like yourself!"

"Devil, cease! Your threats cannot move me!"

"Are you to be happy, while I grovel in wretchedness?"

The Creature is angry and has superhuman strength. He warns Victor that he can make his life a misery.

He gnashes his teeth with rage, and swears that Victor will suffer.

A terrible argument follows!

"Villain!"

"I go—but remember, I shall be with you on your wedding night!"

Victor hurls himself toward the Creature, but he's helpless against the monster's enormous strength and size. The Creature leaves with a terrible threat.

"His words burn in my ears."

"If I return, it is to be sacrificed,[1] or to see those whom I most love die!"

As the Creature rows away, Victor is filled with a frightful feeling of doom. What terrible crimes is the Creature planning for the future?

Victor wanders around the island like a restless ghost. He wishes he could stay there, lonely but safe, forever. He dare not go home.

1. sacrificed: killed.

BURIED AT SEA

Into the sea...

Henry Clerval writes, asking Victor to travel south to join him. But before Victor goes, he must get rid of the unfinished female monster. Shuddering, he loads it into his boat and rows away from shore.

Overcome with relief, Victor falls asleep.

He wakes to find himself at the heart of a raging storm.

At last, the winds and waves calm down, and Victor sees land ahead. He has no idea where he is.

It is the custom of the Irish to hate villains!

He scrambles ashore, only to find himself surrounded and arrested! What's the matter? Why are the fishermen so hostile?

You are to explain about the death of a gentleman who was found murdered here last night.

He has landed at a small fishing port in Ireland. The fishermen march Victor into town, and take him to the magistrate.[1]

It was a very dark night...

They're convinced that Victor's a criminal! The magistrate asks the fishermen to tell their story.

1. magistrate: local judge.

The fishermen explain that last night they found a young man's body on the shore. It was not drowned, but strangled—and still warm! One of them saw a boat sailing away, and it looked just like Victor's.

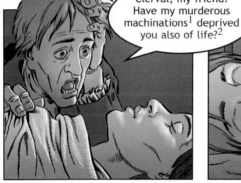

Victor is taken to see the body. He can't believe his eyes. The dead man is his best friend, Henry Clerval, who was travelling north to meet him!

Victor cannot bear to think that the Creature he made has killed Henry. He collapses, unconscious.

Victor is now a prisoner.

I am sorry that I am still alive to feel this misery and horror.

The magistrate visits. He's worried to see Victor so ill, in mind and body. He has written to Victor's father …

A friend is come to visit you.

…who hurries all the way from Geneva to be with him. Victor is overjoyed to see him again. At last he begins to grow stronger.

Are you safe—and Elizabeth—and Ernest?

Destiny[3] of the most horrible kind hangs over me!

But thoughts of Henry's death and the Creature's terrible threats of revenge still fill him with deep despair.

1. murderous machinations: deadly schemes (to make the two creatures).
2. deprived you also of life: killed you, too.
3. Destiny: fate; tragedy still to come.

DEADLY WEDDING

Victor and his father travel slowly back to Geneva. Victor's still ill. He accuses himself of causing the deaths of William, Justine, and Henry. His father has no idea what he means.

When they reach Paris, Victor receives a letter from Elizabeth. She thinks she knows why he put off the marriage.

No! Victor still loves Elizabeth. But the thought of marriage reminds him of the Creature's threat.

Will marriage mean Victor's murder, and yet more sadness caused by the Creature? Weeping, he writes to Elizabeth.

Victor arrives home.

The wedding day arrives. Victor has promised to reveal his secret to Elizabeth the next day. Meanwhile he tries to hide his worries, but secretly carries guns and a dagger.

After the wedding party, Victor and Elizabeth sail away to start their honeymoon. They leave the boat to spend the night in a hotel. Victor's worries return.

1. infatuation: wild idea.
2. the prospect before us: our future.

This night, and all will be safe:[1] but this night is dreadful!

Elizabeth goes to their room. Victor plans to search the hotel, then join her.

Victor finds no trace of the Creature and is beginning to feel safe—when a blood-curdling scream pierces the air!

AIIEEE!

Great God!

My love, my wife— so dear, so worthy!

Elizabeth has been strangled. Victor cradles his wife's lifeless body in his arms—and there is the hideous Creature at the window, enjoying Victor's pain!

Victor fires his gun, but the Creature escapes and leaps into the lake. The villagers give chase as well, but the Creature is too quick for them.

Cursed, cursed be the fiend that brought misery on his grey hairs!

Victor clings to his dead wife, weeping uncontrollably. But then he has a terrible thought. Has the Creature gone to attack his father and brother? Victor rushes back to Geneva, and finds his father dying. The shock of Elizabeth's murder has been too much for him.

1. This night, and all will be safe: After this night, all will be safe.

THE FINAL TRAGEDY

"I would willingly afford[1] you every aid, but..."

"By the sacred earth on which I kneel, I swear to pursue the demon."

"I am satisfied!"

Victor is numb with grief. But at last he decides to take action. He tells the whole story to the local magistrate and demands that the Creature be arrested.

If the law can't help, then Victor must destroy the Creature himself! In the graveyard where William, Elizabeth, and his father are buried, he swears revenge.

Even as Victor speaks, he hears a sickening laugh. The Creature is gloating over the suffering he has caused.

"I am cursed by some devil, and carry about with me eternal hell."

"My life is hateful to me."

Victor chases after him, but the Creature is stronger and faster than any ordinary man.

He tracks the Creature for months, through fields and forests, from Switzerland through Austria, Hungary, and Russia.

Sometimes the Creature taunts Victor by leaving clues to guide him. Half-starving, Victor survives by killing and eating wild beasts.

"Oh blessed sleep!"

The trail leads Victor north, through snow and ice.

"I am gaining on him.[2]"

Only in sleep can Victor get some rest from his nightmare existence. He sees his dead loved ones in his dreams.

1. afford: offer, give.
2. gaining on him: catching up with him.

38

Once he gets near enough to catch sight of the Creature.

But again Victor's hopes are dashed. With a thunderous crash, the Arctic ice cracks and he falls into the sea.

You took me on board when my vigor[1] was exhausted.

He almost freezes to death in the ice-cold water, but, miraculously, Walton's ship appears. Victor is taken on board.

Swear to me, Walton, that he shall not escape.

I believed myself destined for some great enterprise.

Farewell, Walton! Seek happiness in tranquillity,[2] and avoid ambition.

Oh, Frankenstein! I now ask thee to pardon me!

Victor realizes he is close to death. With great difficulty, he whispers some final words of advice to Walton. Then he dies peacefully, hoping to meet his family in heaven.

At midnight, Walton looks into Victor's cabin. Kneeling over Victor's body is a creature he cannot find words to describe.

You hate me, but your abhorrence[3] cannot equal that with which I regard myself.

Soon my spirit will sleep in peace.

Farewell, Frankenstein!

The Creature is finally sorry for all he's done. His good character was turned to bad by misery and loneliness. Now he plans to destroy himself and end his suffering forever.

The end

1. vigor: strength.
2. tranquillity: peace and calm.
3. abhorrence: hatred, disgust.

Mary Wollstonecraft Godwin was born in London, England, on August 30, 1797. Her parents were well-known writers with progressive, shocking ideas. Her mother, Mary Wollstonecraft, wrote a famous book demanding equal rights for women. Her father, William Godwin, was a journalist who believed that England needed a revolution.

Tragically, her mother died when Mary was only ten days old. Godwin was too busy to look after young children, or show them much affection. So, to care for Mary and her half-sister Fanny, he married again. Mary did not like her stepmother, and hated her new stepsister, Jane (known as Claire) Clairmont.

Although he was a cold, distant father, Godwin was proud of Mary. She was an intelligent, thoughtful child—and very pretty—and he encouraged her to read, study, and discuss ideas with the scientists, writers, artists, and philosophers who visited their home. He also let Mary spend long, happy holidays with a Scottish family, the Baxters.

Mary Shelley, about 1840. An engraving based on a painting by Richard Rothwell (1800–1868).

MARY AND PERCY
In 1812, Mary met a new visitor to her father's house, the young, handsome, rebellious poet, Percy Bysshe Shelley. Two years later, Mary and Shelley fell in love and ran away together, leaving Shelley's pregnant wife behind. Mary was 16, Shelley five years older. Their friends were shocked; Godwin was horrified, and refused to speak to Mary for a year.

For six weeks, Mary and Percy travelled through Europe—then returned home in disgrace, with no money. Shelley's father was rich—and a nobleman—but disapproved of Shelley's behavior and stopped his allowance. Mary's first child, a girl, was born in 1815, but soon died. In a disturbing dream, Mary imagined that the child came back to life again. In January 1816, Mary had a son, William.

THE BIRTH OF *FRANKENSTEIN*
Soon afterward, Mary and Shelley—with baby William and stepsister Claire—went to stay in a lakeside cottage near Geneva, Switzerland. Their neighbor was the brilliant, scandalous poet, Lord

Byron. Together they spent a happy, carefree spring, walking in the woods, boating on the lake, reading, talking, and writing. But by midsummer the weather changed, and they were kept indoors by storms.

To pass the time, Byron suggested that they each write a ghost story. For some days, Mary could not think of a plot. Then, late one night in June, in what she called "a waking dream," the idea for *Frankenstein* took shape in her brain. She began to write.

In September 1816, Mary and Shelley returned to England. In December, Shelley's wife was found dead; soon after, Mary and Shelley married. Mary completed *Frankenstein* on May 14, 1817; four months later, she gave birth to a third child, Clara.

Frankenstein was published in January 1818. In March, Mary, Shelley, and their children left England to live and write in Italy. Baby Clara died on their travels; young William died soon after, in June 1819. Their deaths made Mary deeply depressed, but she still kept on writing. In November 1819 she had her last child, a boy named Percy Florence (after his father, Percy Shelley, and the Italian city of Florence, where he was born).

WIDOWED

For the next two years, Mary and Shelley lived happily—and busily—writing, exploring ancient monuments, and visiting friends. Then, in early July 1822, Shelley set off by boat to meet visitors from England. A storm blew in, the boat was wrecked, and Shelley drowned. He was 29; Mary was 24.

Mary was heartbroken, and vowed never to marry again. For the rest of her life she devoted herself to preserving Shelley's memory and looking after their precious child, Percy Florence.

She stayed in Italy until the end of 1823, then returned to London. There, to earn money, she wrote an astonishing number of articles for literary, political, and popular magazines, biographies of famous writers and thinkers, and several novels. She also edited Shelley's poems and wrote his life story— although his father tried to have the book banned.

She remained close to Percy Florence, who survived to adulthood—and enjoyed adventurous foreign holidays with him and his friends. Mary died in 1851, at age 53.

Percy Bysshe Shelley in 1819. An engraving based on a painting by Amelia Curran (d. 1847).

FRANKENSTEIN'S TRAVELS

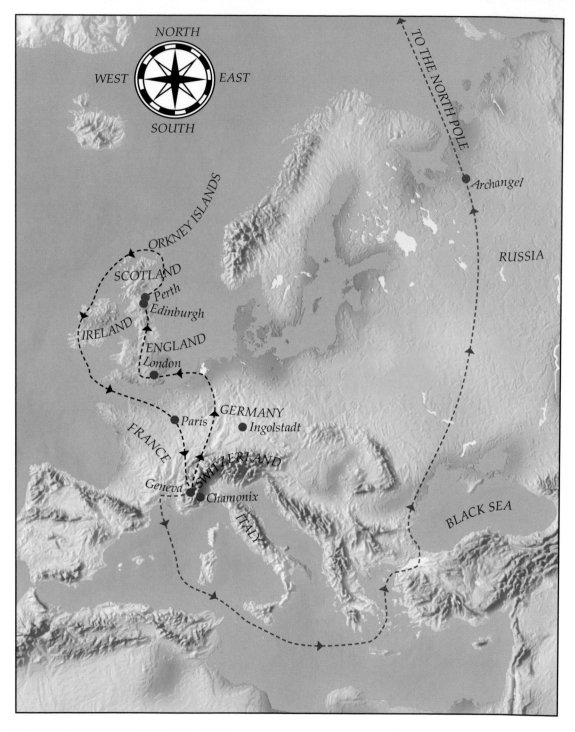

NORTH

WEST · EAST

SOUTH

TO THE NORTH POLE

Archangel

RUSSIA

ORKNEY ISLANDS

SCOTLAND

Perth

Edinburgh

IRELAND

ENGLAND

London

GERMANY

Paris

Ingolstadt

FRANCE

SWITZERLAND

Geneva

Chamonix

ITALY

BLACK SEA

- - - ▶ - - - - ▶ - - - *Victor's journey to Britain and back*
- - - ▶ - - - - ▶ - - - *Victor's chase after the Creature*

For much of her life, Mary Shelley was surrounded by brilliant, famous people. They admired bold, heroic actions, and sometimes ignored the rules of normal good behavior. They were passionately interested in daring experiments and wild new ideas.

Mary shared many of these passions. She was also keenly interested in science and philosophy. But, more clearly than her companions, she realized the damage that wild experiments and revolutions might do. In particular, she worried about the impact of thoughtless, uncontrolled discoveries and inventions.

Mary's concerns are clear in the story of *Frankenstein*. Young Victor uses his intelligence and enthusiasm to make a new, living Creature. But he lacks the knowledge, wisdom, and sense of responsibility to care for it or control it. Instead, he runs away and tries to forget about it. Mary does not condemn Victor, or praise him. She leaves her readers to decide whether Victor's actions are good or bad. She makes us think!

THEN AND NOW

Today, some people have similar worries about the uncontrolled development of medicine, science, and technology. They use the story of *Frankenstein* to draw attention to their fears. They describe polluting machines and hard-to-kill germs as "monsters," and genetically modified crops as "Frankenstein foods."

So, in some ways, Mary's book is as up to date now as it was when she wrote it nearly 200 years ago.

SUBLIME SCENERY

Like many writers of her time, Mary Shelley believed that landscape had the power to mold people's characters and influence their actions. In particular, huge, beautiful lakes and mountains, like those of Frankenstein's Switzerland, could raise human thoughts to a "sublime" (superhuman) level, and bring them nearer to God. In her books, Mary Shelley also used landscape, natural events such as storms and lightning, and bleak, dangerous locations, such as the Arctic, to mirror states of excitement, terror, or misery in her characters' minds.

Part of the Mer de Glace ("Sea of Ice") near Chamonix, France. Mary Shelley visited this spectacular glacier in 1816 and used it as the setting for the first fateful conversation between Victor Frankenstein and his Creature (see page 23).

SCIENTIFIC DISCOVERIES

MEDICINE AND ELECTRICITY AT THE TIME OF *FRANKENSTEIN*

Mary Shelley liked to read the latest scientific books as soon as they were published. She would have known about many of the following inventions and discoveries at the time she was writing *Frankenstein* (1818) and revising it (between 1823 and 1831).

1747
Lightning conductor invented by U.S. scientist Benjamin Franklin. He makes many studies to investigate electricity.

1760s
European and U.S. farmers experiment with selective breeding of cows, sheep, and pigs to improve their size and appearance.

1761
System of percussion (tapping on chest to diagnose illness) invented by Austrian doctor Leopold Auenbrugger.

1766
Action of nerve impulses (electrical signals) to control muscle action (and therefore movement) is discovered by Swiss scientist Albrecht von Haller.

1768
Scientific method of experimental pathology (cutting up dead bodies to help understand living ones) is invented by Scottish doctor John Hunter.

1770
Composition of bones discovered by Swedish scientist Johan Gahn.

1771
Blood clotting investigated by British doctor William Hensen.

1772
Inner structure of the ear discovered by Italian doctor Antonio Scarpa.

1772 and 1774
Oxygen—the gas needed for breathing by most living creatures—discovered by Swedish scientist Karl Scheele and British scientist Joseph Priestley.

1773
Digestive action of saliva discovered by Italian Lazzaro Spallanzani.

1780s
British "quack" (fraud) doctor James Graham sets up "Temple of Health" to offer treatments based on electricity and magnetism. They include a "celestial" (heavenly) bed, which Graham claims will help couples create children.

1781
Chemical composition of water (essential for human, animal, and plant life) discovered by British scientist Henry Cavendish.

1783
Italian scientist Luigi Galvani investigates the effects of electricity on dead creatures' muscles. It makes them move. Galvani called this movement "animal electricity"; it later became known as "galvanism." He believes (wrongly) that electricity is an invisible fluid, flowing from animals' muscles (flesh) to their nerves.

1794
First ideas about animal evolution suggested by British doctor Erasmus Darwin (grandfather of Charles Darwin).

1795–1796
American quack doctor Elisha Perkins invents metal rods called "metallic tractors." He claims these will draw off poisonous "electrical fluid" that he says causes suffering.

1796
British doctor Edward Jenner pioneers vaccination against smallpox. Many people fear that it will produce monsters.

1799
Mass-production system for manufacturing all kinds of objects invented in England by French-born engineer Marc Brunel.

1799
Experiments with anesthetic gases by British scientists Thomas Beddoes and Humphry Davy.

1800
First electric battery, the "voltaic pile," invented by Italian scientist Alessandro Volta.

1800
Electrolysis of water (splitting it into separate components, using electric current) discovered by British chemists William Nicholson and Anthony Carlisle.

1802
Storage / rechargeable battery invented by German scientist Johann Ritter.

1802
Pioneer British experimental scientist Humphry Davy publishes *Lectures on Chemistry*.

1803
Theory that all matter is made of tiny particles, called atoms, is suggested by British scientist John Dalton.

1803
Painkilling drug morphine discovered by French chemist Charles Derosne.

1803
Italian doctor Giovanni Aldini experiments with electricity on dead bodies of criminals, trying, but failing, to bring them back to life.

1806
First-known amino acid (protein used to build and repair human tissues) discovered by French chemists Louis Vauquelin and Pierre Robiquet.

1807
British scientist Thomas Young works out how to measure the elasticity of any substance.

1809
French scientist Jean-Baptiste Lamarck suggests (wrongly) that learned characteristics and behavior can be inherited.

1811
Fossil bones of a giant "monster" (an ichthyosaur) found in England.

1811
Sensory nerves (that feel) and motor nerves (that send movement messages to muscles) are discovered by Scottish doctor Charles Bell.

1812
Humphry Davy publishes a very important book: *Elements of Chemical Philosophy*.

1817
Dental plate (modern false teeth) invented by U.S. dentist Anthony Plantson.

1818
Homeopathy invented by German doctor Samuel Hahnemann. He believe that minute doses of substances that cause illness could help the body cure disease.

1820
Electromagnetism (production of a magnetic field by an electric current) discovered by Danish scientist Hans Oersted.

1823
Composition of human and animal fat investigated by French scientist Michel Chevreul.

1825
Giant "monster" (fossil dinosaur) teeth found in England.

1826
Improved microscope invented by British biologist James Smith, with lenses designed by British investigator Joseph Lister. It helps scientists study details of living things too small for the naked eye to see.

1828
German scientist Friedrich Wohler makes an organic chemical (normally found in living creatures) from an inorganic one (normally found in non-living substances).

1828
Improved stethoscope invented by French doctor Pierre Poirry. It allows scientists and doctors to listen to the hearts and lungs of living, breathing people.

1831
Anesthetic gas chloroform is discovered by scientists in Germany, Britain, and France. It makes patients unconscious for a while, so doctors can operate on them.

1831
Electromagnetic induction (way of producing an electric current by changing a magnetic field) is discovered by British scientist Michael Faraday.

1832
Nerve reflexes (jerky, automatic movements) are discovered by English doctor Marshall Hall.

1833
Enzymes (chemical messengers and transformers) are discovered by French chemists Anselme Payen and Jean-François Persoz.

1834
Carbolic acid, a powerful disinfectant later used by doctors to stop germs spreading during operations, is discovered by German chemist Friedlieb Runge.

1817
History of a Six Weeks' Tour, the story of Mary's travels when she first ran away with Percy Shelley.

1819
Mathilda, a short novel about fathers and daughters.

1821
Castruccio (later called *Valperga*), a dramatic, romantic novel.

1824
Posthumous Poems (an edition of poems that Percy Shelley left unpublished when he died).

1824–1839
Very many magazine articles.

1826
The Last Man, a novel set in the 21st century. The story of the only man to survive a world epidemic.

1830
The Fortunes of Perkin Warbeck, a historical novel about a 15th-century pretender to the English throne.

1835
Lodore, a novel featuring a hero who breaks society's rules. Based on elements of Percy Shelley's character and life story.

1835–1839
Biographies of important European writers and thinkers, for *Lardner's Cabinet Cyclopaedia* (that is, brief encyclopedia).

1837
Falkner, Mary Shelley's last novel. Also based in part on the life and ideas of Mary's late husband, Percy Bysshe Shelley.

1839
Mary edits Percy Shelley's *Poetical Works*, and adds details of his life story. Also edits Shelley's *Essays, Letters and Translations*.

1844
Rambles in Germany and Italy, the story of Mary's European travels with Percy Florence, her son.

The awakening of the Creature as shown in an engraving by Chevalier in the 1831 edition of Frankenstein.

FRANKENSTEIN FILMS

Mary Shelley's novel gripped the public imagination as soon as it appeared. Within just five years (1823), it had been turned into a stage play. Mary went to see it, but commented that "the story was not well managed." By 1826, fifteen different stage versions of *Frankenstein* were being performed. All of them changed the thought-provoking "message" of Mary's book. *Frankenstein* became either a simplified story of good versus evil, or else a dramatic "shocker," full of thoughtless, brutal violence.

When films were invented, in the late 19th century, *Frankenstein* appealed to filmmakers as well. The first *Frankenstein* film was made in 1910. It was short, silent, and in black and white. Since then, over 800 film versions of the *Frankenstein* story have appeared. Some present Victor Frankenstein as a mad scientist, driven by ruthless ambition to create life, even if it destroys the world. Others portray the Creature as mindless, destructive—and programmed to kill. They glory in scenes of bloodshed and suffering.

In spite of this, a few *Frankenstein* films have won praise as works of art and entertainment in their own right. They include:

1931: *Frankenstein* (USA)
Stars Boris Karloff as a cruel, stupid, speechless monster. Introduces the well-known image of the Creature with flat head and bolts through the neck.

1957: *The Curse of Frankenstein* (UK)
A Hammer Horror film starring charismatic Peter Cushing as evil scientist Victor Frankenstein.

Boris Karloff as the Creature in a 1930s film.

1974: *Young Frankenstein* (USA)
A spoof, directed by Mel Brooks, in which Victor Frankenstein's grandson creates a particularly stupid monster.

1994: *Mary Shelley's Frankenstein* (UK)
Directed by Kenneth Branagh, with Robert De Niro as the Creature, this film keeps a little closer to the original story than most other versions.

Other famous films about man-made monsters include:

1926: *Metropolis* (Germany)
Mixes *Frankenstein*, science fiction, and politics. Features a female robot who leads a rebellion against her makers to help the poor.

1982: *Blade Runner* (USA)
Set in the future, when man-made robots threaten the world. Stars action hero Harrison Ford.

1987 *RoboCop* (USA)
Very violent. Features a cyborg protagonist, half-man, half-machine.

INDEX

FURTHER INFORMATION

IF YOU ENJOYED THIS BOOK, YOU MIGHT LIKE TO TRY
THESE OTHER TITLES IN THE BARRON'S *GRAPHIC CLASSICS* SERIES:

Dracula by Bram Stoker
The Hunchback of Notre Dame by Victor Hugo
Journey to the Center of the Earth by Jules Verne
Kidnapped by Robert Louis Stevenson
Macbeth by William Shakespeare
The Man in the Iron Mask by Alexandre Dumas
Moby-Dick by Herman Melville
Oliver Twist by Charles Dickens
Treasure Island by Robert Louis Stevenson

FOR MORE INFORMATION ON MARY SHELLEY AND
FRANKENSTEIN:

en.wikipedia.org/wiki/Mary_Shelley
www.kirjasto.sci.fi/mshelley.htm
people.brandeis.edu/~teuber/shelleybio.html
home-3.tiscali.nl/~hamberg/